Stories Without Words

www.enchantedlionbooks.com

First American Edition published in 2011 by
Enchanted Lion Books LLC, 20 Jay Street, Studio M-18, Brooklyn, NY 11201
Translation copyright © 2011 by Enchanted Lion Books
Originally published in France by Éditions Autrement © 2011 as
Partie de pêche by Béatrice Rodriguez
All rights reserved under International and Pan-American Copyright Conventions
Library of Congress Control Number: 2010942699 ISBN 978-1-59270-109-4
Printed in January 2011 in China by South China Printing Co. Ltd., King Yip
(Dong Guan) Printing & Packaging Factory Co. Ltd., Daning Administrative District,
Humen Town, Dong Guan City, Guangdong Province 523930

Fox and Hen Together

BÉATRICE RODRIGUEZ

ENCHANTED LION BOOKS
NEW YORK

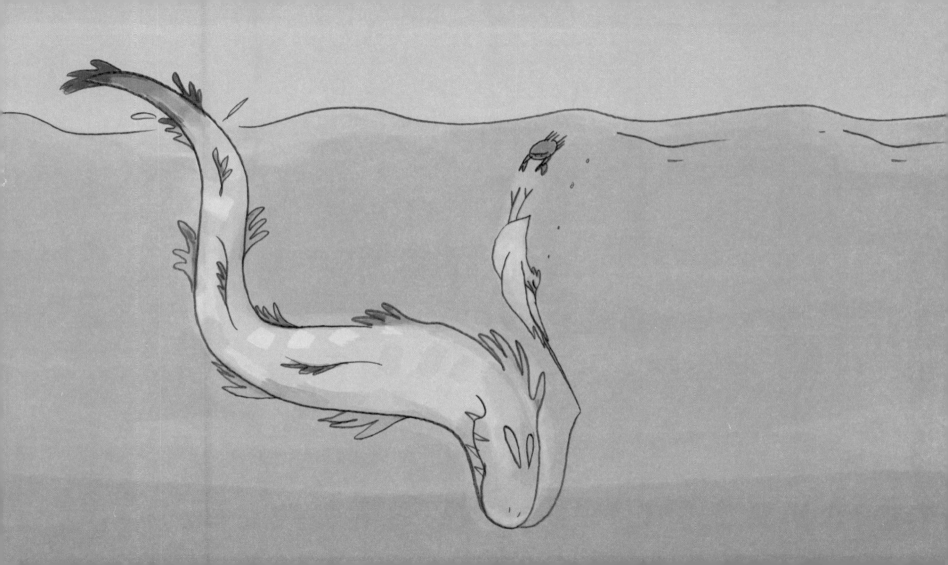